PRIMARILY PORTFOLIOS

Linda Karges-Bone, Ed.D. and Veronica Terrill

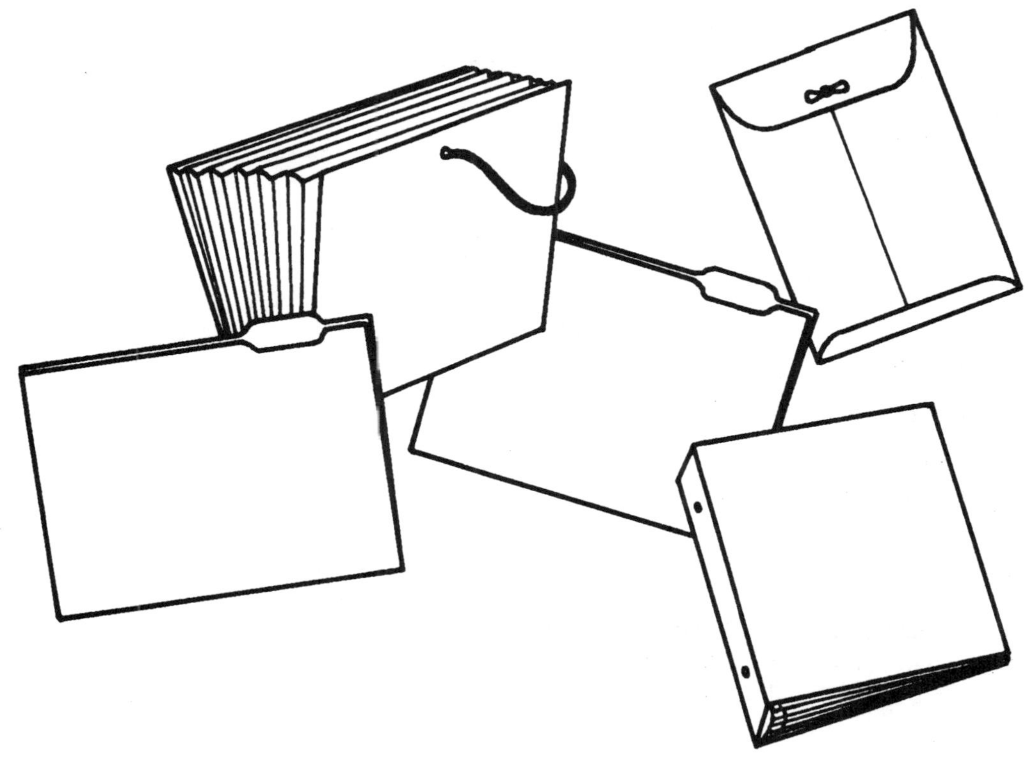

Good Apple
A Division of Frank Schaffer Publications, Inc.

Dedication

This book is for A.J. When I gather up the pages of my life's portfolio, you will be found on the happiest ones. Thank you.
1 John 4:7

Linda Karges-Bone

To my earth angels—my husband Eric, my son Drew, and my daughter Chelsea. I'll love you forever.

Veronica Terrill

Acknowledgments

Special thanks to Carolyn and Audrey Bone for "trying out" the student work pages and letting us know if they made sense to children. The authors also wish to thank Carolea Williams for her enthusiastic support of creative teaching materials with substance.

Executive Editor: Carolea Williams

Editor: Susan Eddy

Cover and Inside Illustration: Veronica Terrill

Cover and Inside Design: Terry McGrath

ISBN 0-86653-853-4

Printed in the United States of America

1 . 9 8 7

Table of Contents

Introduction

Portfolio assessment is the collection of student work over time for the purpose of evaluating knowledge proficiency and measuring growth. It has emerged as a significant trend in the 1990s and is relevant to today's classroom for several important reasons.

Students, teachers, and parents are all beneficiaries of this form of assessment. Students work with a variety of tasks and materials in their area of strength. They take responsibility for the quality of their work and stretch to achieve high levels of cognition. Teachers gain insight into children's strengths and weaknesses as they observe their participation in creative tasks. They find out what children really "know" and can provide masses of meaningful documentation for parents and other faculty. Parents witness growth as well as grades through concrete examples of their child's thinking and knowing. Through participation in portfolio postcard and portfolio partner activities, parents can enhance their child's strength areas in the home.

Primarily Portfolios provides both direction and support for primary teachers who want to begin using portfolios for assessment, whether they are implementing a school-wide system or simply trying out portfolios in one subject area. Portfolio assessment is offered as a complement to more traditional methods of assessment which still serve a purpose and have a place in your battery of assessment tools. By keeping your portfolio system simple and user-friendly and by involving parents and students, portfolios can prove to be a rewarding and enlightening addition to your classroom.

What Is Portfolio Assessment?

The following chart compares portfolio assessment to more traditional forms of assessment.

Portfolio vs. Traditional Assessment

Portfolio Assessment	Traditional Assessment
Takes place over time	Utilizes one test on one day
Includes a variety of samples: drawing, writing, checklists	Limited to one kind of test
Uses rubrics or rating scales to report progress	Uses grades to report progress
Gives students option of selecting best work for portfolio	Gives students few options regarding test-taking
Builds over the course of the school year or years	Isolates assessment—makes few connections over time
Demonstrates multiple intelligences	Demonstrates one kind of intelligence
Stimulates high levels of creativity and divergent thinking	Often demands one "right" answer and convergent thinking
Can assess integrated units of study	Typically measures knowledge in one area only

Two Kinds of Portfolios

At this point, it is helpful to distinguish between the two kinds of portfolios.

Portfolios for Work in Progress

Teachers gather many examples of student work over time for this portfolio and do not remove or sort out products that are weak or need improvement. Students may select a few best products for this portfolio but they are also aware that their other efforts will be included to show progress. This portfolio:

- ✦ Is designed to show improvement over time.
- ✦ Collects more products and, therefore, requires more space but shows growth clearly.
- ✦ Is essential for writing, especially in the early grades. It is good for math as well.
- ✦ Gives parents a more concrete and longitudinal view of progress but the quantity of products may be confusing.

Portfolios for Best Products

Teachers help students select their best products for inclusion in this portfolio. The collection of work remains in the portfolio for a longer duration than it might for the work-in-progress portfolio—possibly for a number of years. This portfolio:

- ✦ Is designed to showcase a student's outstanding efforts.
- ✦ Includes fewer products and therefore requires less space.
- ✦ Is suited to all subject areas.
- ✦ Represents a child's best efforts for parental review—not the totality of work.

What Kind of Portfolio Is Best?

The answer might be whatever suits your needs, your style of organization, the beliefs and attitudes of your parent population, and the availability of storage space in the classroom. It is, of course, possible to use both types of portfolios. Make the decision early in the year for best results. You may wish to sit down with the other teachers in your grade level and discuss reasons for using one type over another—or both. It is always advisable to have as much continuity as possible across a grade level when introducing performance-based or authentic assessment to parents.

Portfolio assessment may make teachers more vulnerable to questions about their academic rigor and standards. Be careful about what goes into portfolios—even "work in progress" portfolios. Encourage students to do their best at all times. Set standards for neatness and appearance. Such practices do not squelch creativity—they help build a sense of achievement. Don't be concerned about damaging a child's self-esteem by setting high standards for work. Self-esteem grows through working hard and achieving goals. Set your standards high in the classroom and watch as students reach for those standards and, eventually, move beyond them. The poster on the following page can be duplicated and displayed in your classroom as a consistent reminder of the standards and goals for portfolio work.

PORTFOLIO CHECKLIST

1. Sign and date your work.

2. Use your best handwriting.

3. Check your work carefully.

4. Use all the information you can think of.

5. Use information in new ways.

6. Work carefully and slowly.

7. Create a product you can be proud of.
   Remember that it represents you.

Preparing for Portfolio Assessment

Before you begin using portfolio assessment in your classroom, give some thought to the organization of the system you will use and the method of collection and storage of portfolios and supplies. Some suggestions for all these areas appear below.

Supplies

Containers for Student Work

(choose one or several of the following, depending on your needs)

- ✦ plastic storage bins
- ✦ accordion files
- ✦ large manila envelopes
- ✦ recycled mailers
- ✦ photo albums
- ✦ pocket folders
- ✦ binders

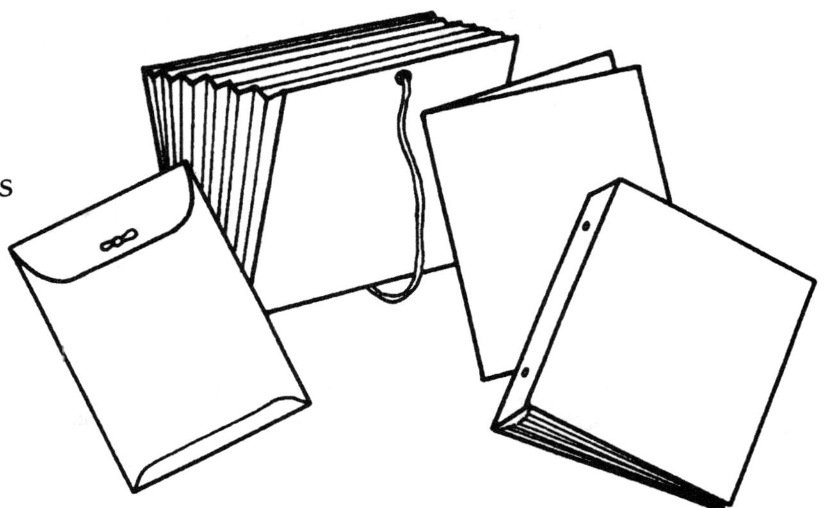

Date Stamps and Stamp Pads

(encourage students to date each item they place in their portfolio)

- ✦ one stamp and pad per every five students
- ✦ ribbons or spiral wire anchors to prevent "walking" date stamps

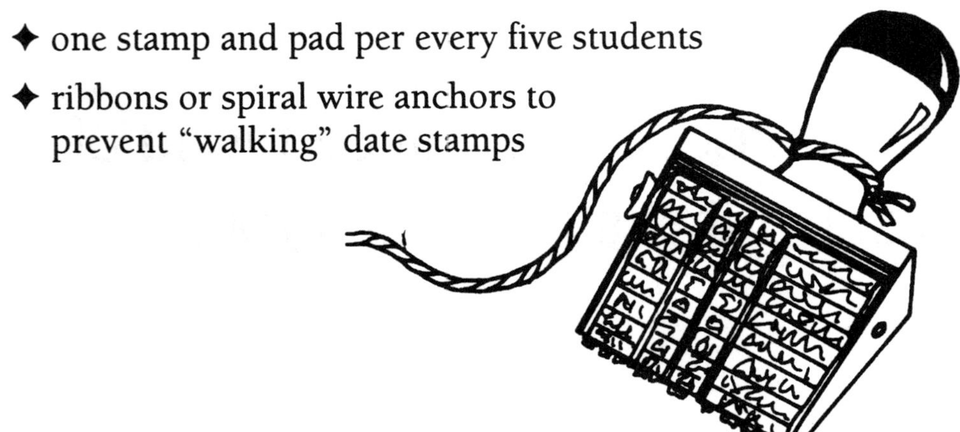

Display Student Work

Think of your classroom as a giant, ever-changing portfolio-in-the-round. Few things make a classroom seem more child-friendly than terrific displays of student products. Extend the display into other locations in the school if possible. Since you are sending less work home, it is vital to the success of your program to keep these displays updated in order to reflect student progress and open up dialogue with other teachers. Pages 19-30 contain six fresh ideas for displaying student work on bulletin boards. Eventually, the work will move into portfolios. Consider the following locations as well.

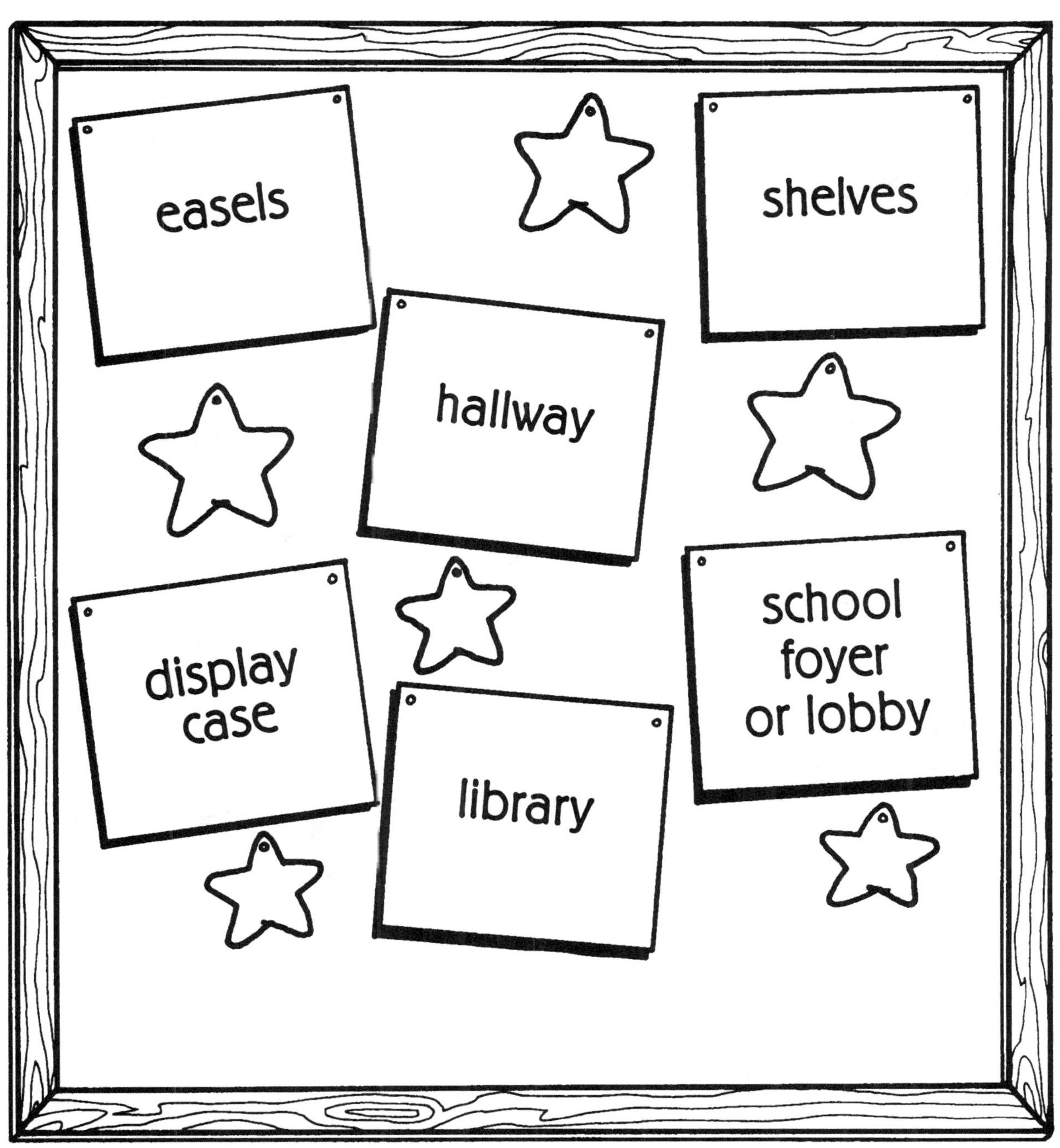

Storage Options

Storage always presents a challenge to teacher creativity. There are lots of options for portfolio storage. The key is to have portfolios easily accessible so that a student doesn't disturb others in the retrieval process. Ideally, students will be able to access their own portfolio without handling everyone else's. Consider the following locations or invite students to devise a storage system for your classroom.

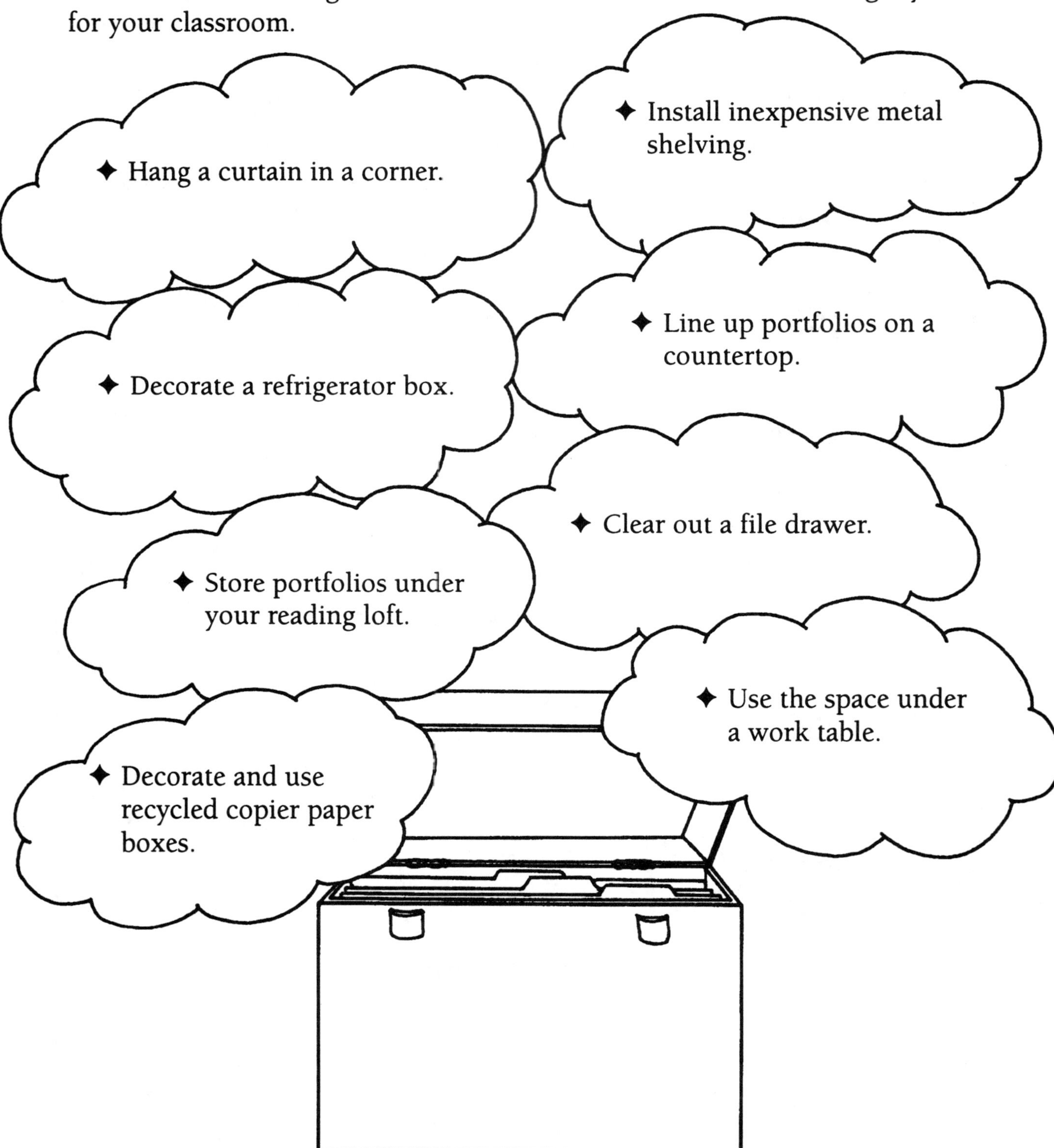

Create a Portfolio Center

If space allows, you may choose to create a Portfolio Center in your classroom to facilitate the organization process. This would be a good place for the classroom poster (see page 9) as well as a sample of work you have assigned for the week. Include copies of the student roster and encourage students to check their names off when the "paper of the week" or selected assignments are safely in their portfolios. (This helps you out as well!) Include sticky notes, pencils, and date stamps at the center. Store the portfolios in boxes or low file drawers. Stacking paper trays can hold generic journal forms, "Personal Favorite" forms, and "Best Work" forms.

Time and Money-Saving Tips

Like many professionals, teachers almost always lack sufficient time and money to accomplish everything they'd like to. Don't let that stop you from trying portfolio assessment. Here are some ways you can save both time and money as you set up your portfolio system.

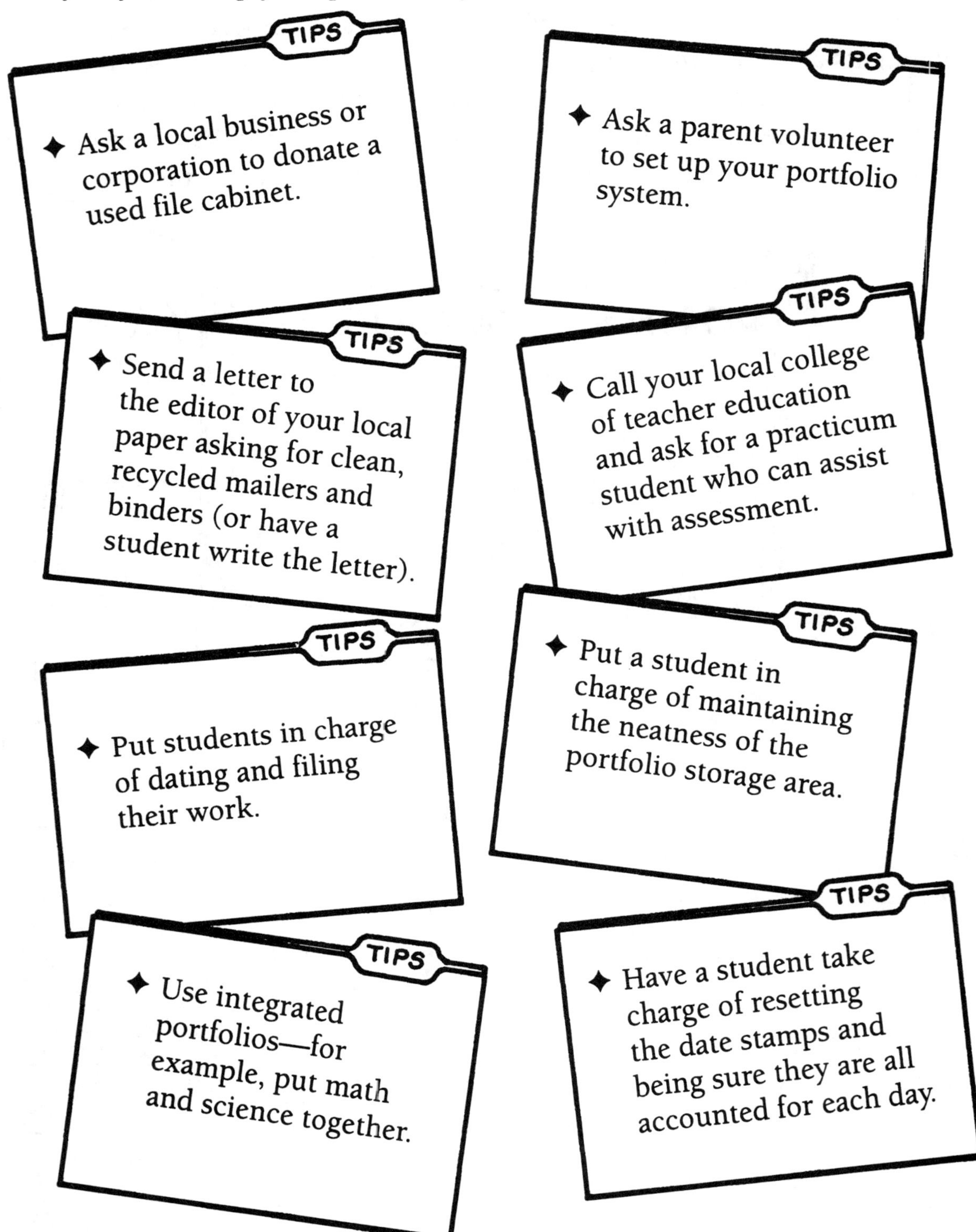

Classroom Management

With a little planning, portfolio assessment can become an integral part of your classroom without a wholesale reshuffling of your current procedures. Build portfolio assessment right into your existing classroom management system. Here are some things to keep in mind as you do this.

- ✦ Send home a letter to parents during the first week of school. Get parents involved—or at least get them behind your efforts. A sample letter is provided on page 16.
- ✦ Display student work frequently and with flair. Students will be eager to participate. Some display ideas are provided on pages 19-30.
- ✦ Praise children for handling the portfolios with care. Convey the idea that portfolios are serious by using the student contract form provided on page 48.
- ✦ Use the portfolio postcards on page 17 or the portfolio partners review form on page 18 to keep families involved with the process and products.
- ✦ Include portfolios in your open house at the beginning of the year.
- ✦ Plan a portfolio party at the end of the year to celebrate excellent work and thank volunteer helpers. See page 96 for more ideas and an invitation.

Sample Parent Letter

Dear Parents,

Did you know that artists are not the only people who use portfolios? Your child and I will be putting together a portfolio of his or her work during the school year. We use portfolios to save and organize student work and to review it over the course of time.

Some of the work will have traditional grades and some will be evaluated in a new way. I will use a rubric and checklist to rate your child's performance. Rubrics and checklists are rating scales that tell us more about a product than simply if the answers are correct. They also tell us more about your child's strengths, talents, and needs. They take into consideration creativity, problem-solving ability, and effort.

Please stop by and see the portfolios as they grow. Take a look at the displays around our classroom. Read the portfolio postcards and portfolio partners review forms that come home and you will get an idea of what is being saved in portfolios. Don't be concerned if it seems that less work is being sent home this year–it is being saved here. Through portfolio assessment, you and I can get a better idea of how much your child has learned and understood.

Please feel free to call me at ___________ if you have any questions.

Yours truly,

Portfolio Postcard

Duplicate this "postcard" on construction paper. Students may write their parents' name on the address side and fill out the message side with information copied from the board or supplied on their own. Invite them to draw a picture of their favorite activity of the week on the picture side.

PORTFOLIO POSTCARD

Dear ____________

Here's what I put in my portfolio this week.

Portfolio Partners Review

Use this form for individual papers or an entire portfolio. Write a student's name in the blank box and invite him or her to comment on the work.

Comments

Parents

Comments

Teacher

Comments

Date________________

Portfolio Paper of the Week

Choose one paper or project to highlight as "Portfolio Paper of the Week." Invite the author to create a self-portrait to accompany his or her work. Add a comment from the student in a word balloon.

1. Cover bulletin board with bright paper and add the title.
2. Mount the portfolio paper on paper of a contrasting color and place on bulletin board.
3. Invite student to add a self-portrait, signature sample, and a comment about the paper you have selected. Add each to the bulletin board as shown.

Hint: You may wish to reward the author of the "Portfolio Paper of the Week" with a special treat or privilege, such as lunch with the teacher, pencils, or stickers.

©1995 GOOD APPLE

Steps to a Great Portfolio

Use this bulletin board early in the year to help students understand expectations. Use examples and descriptions of what you require with footprints forming a path to excellence.

1. Cover bulletin board with bright paper and add the title.
2. Reproduce the patterns on page 22 and any other sample sheets you plan to include as "steps."
3. Number each footprint and add any important information you feel is necessary. Add each to the bulletin board as shown.

Hint: You may wish to reduce the filled-in footprints to four inches in length and use them as handouts for students. This will help them keep track of the steps they have completed.

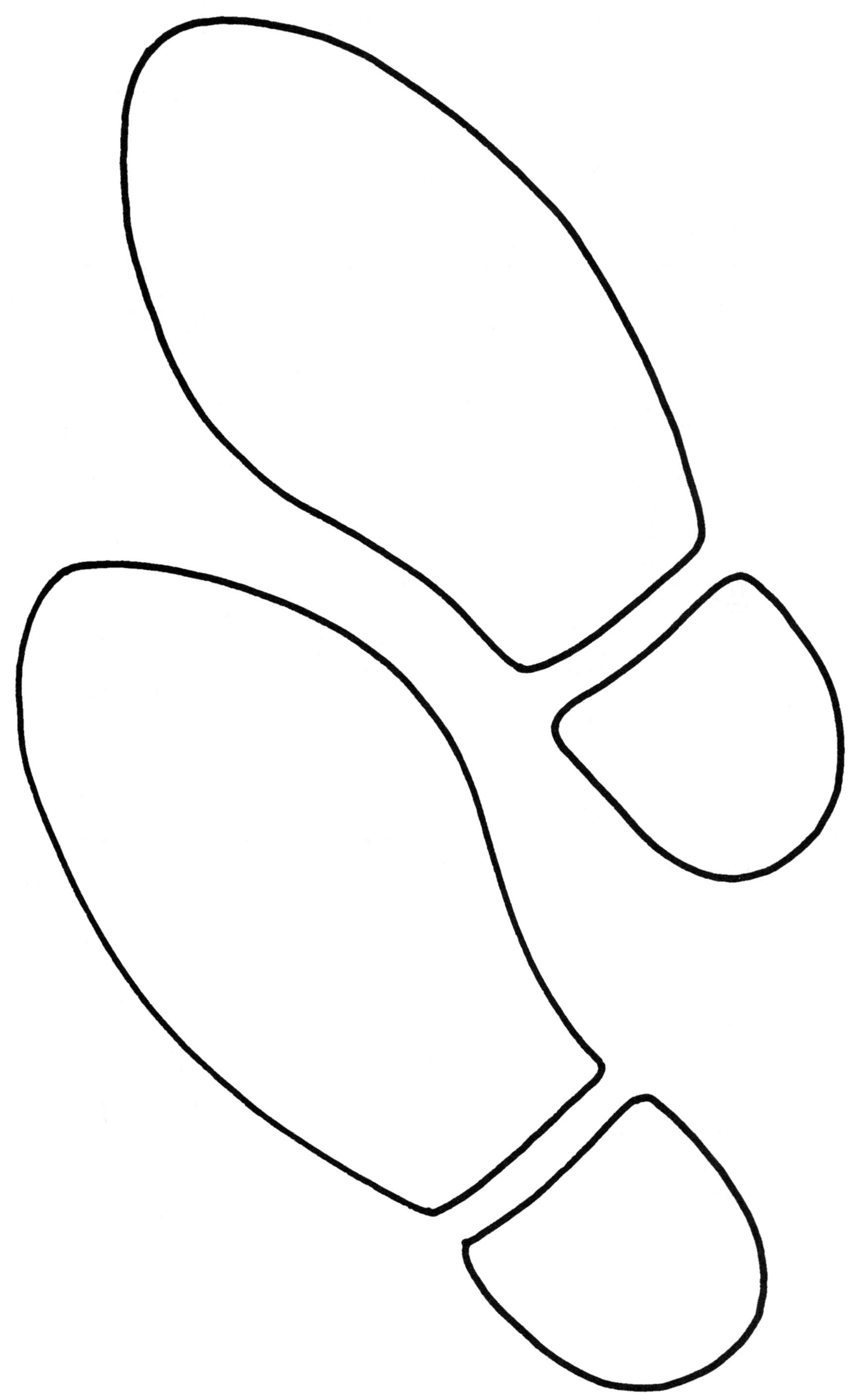

Monthly Masterpieces

This art-related display can remain in your classroom all year. Change the creations monthly for a revolving art gallery.

1. Cover the bulletin board with abstractly-shaped areas of colored paper and add the title.
2. Reproduce and enlarge the pattern on page 24. Color and place on bulletin board.
3. Display student artwork as illustrated.

Hint: You may wish to make construction paper "frames" for each piece of artwork you display to give each one a more finished look.

Purr-fect Portfolio Papers

When there are many wonderful pieces of work to share, use this display.

1. Cover bulletin board with bright paper and add the title.
2. Reproduce the patterns on page 26 and cut out. Color the paw prints in various bright shades.
3. Attach kittens to portfolio papers and display on bulletin board with paw prints.

Hint: You may wish to use copies of the paw print as reward coupons. Students may redeem a certain number of paw prints for a prize, such as a pencil.

CUT ON DOTTED LINES AND INSERT PAPER

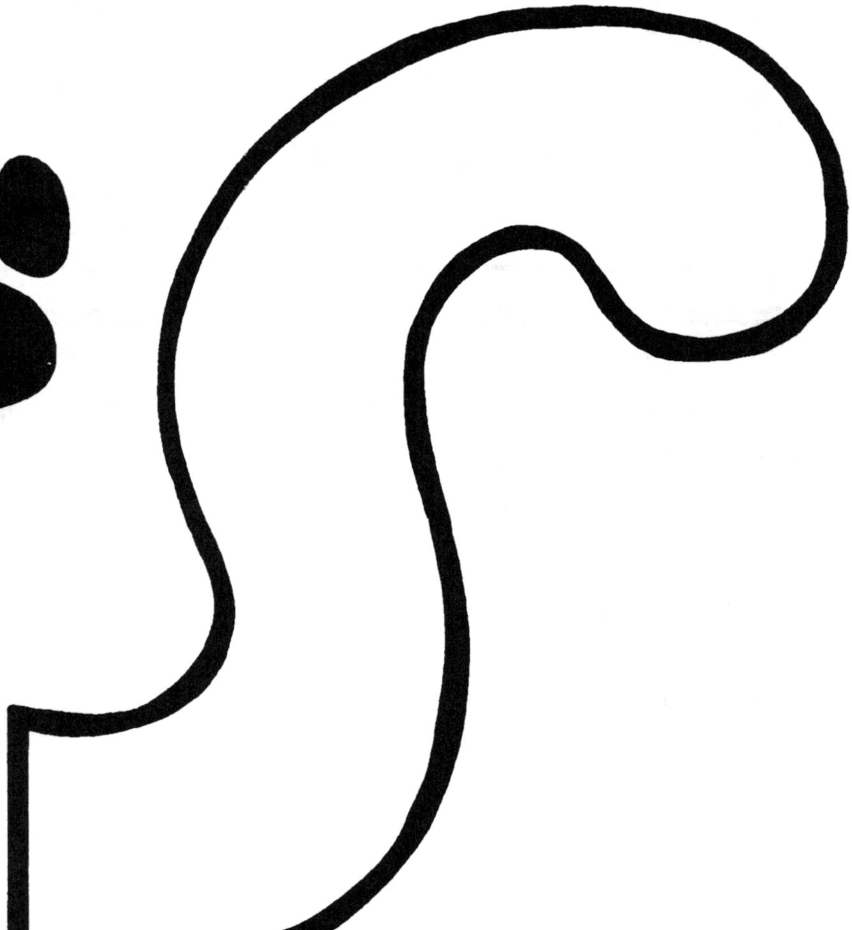

Portfolio Partners

This bulletin board can be used to highlight the work of two individuals as well as their work as a team.

1. Cover bulletin board with bright paper and add the title.
2. Enlarge and color pattern on page 28 and place on bulletin board.
3. Using colorful yarn, create two overlapping lassos on the bulletin board as illustrated.
4. Add portfolio papers. Team projects are displayed in the overlapping space.

Hint: Celebrate the portfolio partnership with matching awards, such as badges or stickers.

Sweet Success

Create an end-of-year display complete with colorful balloons, "candy," and confetti. This bulletin board makes a festive backdrop if you decide to have a year-end portfolio party (see page 96).

1. Cover bulletin board with bright paper and add the title.
2. Reproduce the patterns on page 30 on colorful paper. Invite the principal, other teachers, and students to add their messages on the balloons.
3. Place "candy" with names added and balloons on bulletin board as illustrated.
4. Add small, colorful triangles of paper for confetti.

Hint: You might send small copies of the balloon home to parents in a sealed envelope and invite them to personalize the balloons as a surprise for students at the party.

©1995 GOOD APPLE

Organizing Portfolio Assessment

Now that you've made the decision to try portfolio assessment, you probably have some "nuts and bolts" questions about how the process functions. The following information should answer those questions. Keep in mind, however, that every system of portfolio assessment is tailored to the specific needs of you—the teacher, your program, and your physical space. Feel free to adapt and modify wherever necessary but don't lose sight of the fact that portfolios are for assessment, not merely storage.

What goes in the portfolio?

You can collect one or two items each week or one or two items each day—your options are wide open. Use the content checklists at the beginning of each subject area section to help you determine what might be included in a math, language arts, or science portfolio. The idea is to show growth over time as well as a variety of student work. Include drawings, writing, worksheets, individual tasks, and small group tasks. Portfolio assessment can be used with more traditional forms of assessment as well. Chapter tests, quizzes, and achievement test results can go into a portfolio right next to writing samples and journals. When you evaluate students' work, every little bit helps paint a clearer picture.

How long does work stay in a portfolio?

To show growth over time, a portfolio should be created over the course of the school year. Ideally, writing portfolios will move from grade to grade with the student during the first six years of school. It is not necessary to keep everything—just examples of a student's work. Many papers will still be sent home in the traditional fashion. If you opt to do thematic unit portfolios, the work can be sent home at the end of the unit. Obviously when portfolios become unwieldy, some organization and clean-out is warranted. Meet with your students to review the contents of the portfolio and help them decide what to keep and what to take home. A simple table of contents stapled to the front of each portfolio can help keep both student and teacher organized (see pages 39-43).

How and when do you meet with parents concerning portfolios?

This will vary according to the requirements of the school and community. Strive to meet with parents once each quarter to review the contents of the portfolio—more often if the child is experiencing problems. Focus on specific areas of strength or weakness using the checklists as a guide. Be sure to use the portfolio conference sheet on page 36 for organization and record-keeping purposes. Portfolios are for sharing and in portfolio assessment, conferences serve as an additional reporting tool. Parents appreciate the positive feedback and specific information concerning weaker areas of their child's performance.

What are rubrics and checklists?

Rubrics are descriptions of performance. They give specific guidelines or descriptors of how the different levels of performance—novice, standard, expert—might "look." Checklists outline the specific skills or abilities you are using the rubric to assess. You assign each skill a performance level right on the checklist. For example, a student might be a novice in reading fluency and an expert counter. Examples of both rubrics and checklists are included in each subject area section, as well as some filled-in samples. Checklists and rubrics complete the assessment cycle and make the system work. Take time at the beginning of the year to explain the rubrics and checklists to your students—it is important that they understand how you will be approaching assessment. Make your expectations clear. Help them understand the principle of "growth over time" and that this idea in fact releases them from some of the pressure numerical grades may create. And—most importantly—spend some time conferencing with your students once you have assessed their work. Explain to them what you have learned from the assessment and get their input. Students love this one-on-one experience and the feedback is important for both of you. Try to find the time to meet with each student at least once a month.

What about report cards?

If your school requires a traditional report card with letter or number grades, assign a number or letter to each category of your rubrics. Simply average the grades at report card time as you have always done. These traditional grades need not appear in the portfolio at all—they are strictly for required record keeping. Another option is to give a traditional report card with an enclosure or progress report in more "authentic" terms. A sample portfolio progress enclosure form appears on page 35.

Flow Chart for Portfolio Assessment

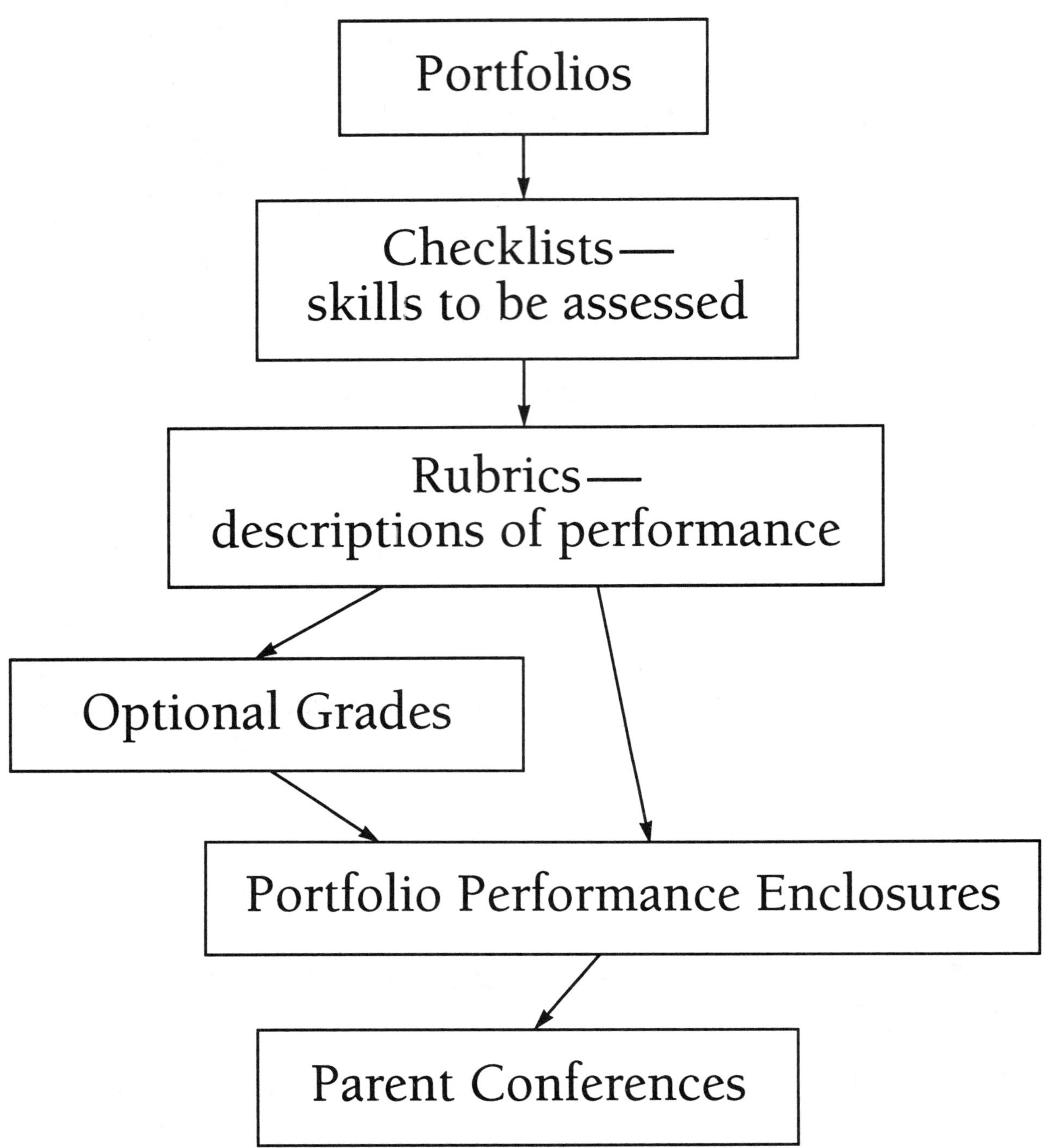

Portfolio Progress Enclosure Form

Name ______________________________ Date ________________

Type of portfolio: ____

Assessment period: From _______________ to __________________

Teacher ________________________ School __________________

✦ ✦

During this period of assessment, your child's overall progress can best be described as ____

____

Specifically, in the area(s) of ______________________________, your child shows high levels of ability. The following tasks from the portfolio offer examples of this ability.

____

____

In the area(s) of ____________________________________, your child's performance indicates some weakness or difficulty. The following tasks from the portfolio offer examples of this weakness.

____

Based on my assessment of your child's work during this period, his or her learning style can best be described as

VISUAL AUDITORY TACTILE

Your child's work habits can best be described as

STRONG AVERAGE WEAK

Portfolio Conference Sheet

Child's name ____________________ Date of conference ___________

Assessment period: From _________________ to ________________

Teacher ____________________ School _________________________

✦ ✦

Issues discussed ____

____

____

Specific strengths ____

____

____

Specific weaknesses ____

____

____

Concerns raised by parents ____________________________________

____

Plan for assisting student _____________________________________

____

____

Parent's signature __________________________ Date ____________

Teacher's signature _________________________ Date ____________

Principal's signature ________________________ Date ____________

Using Portfolio Assessment Across the Curriculum

Portfolio assessment is flexible and adaptable. You can use portfolios for integrated or thematic units of study, you can combine subject areas, or you may choose to use them in only one subject area if you are just getting started. The following information will help you decide how portfolio assessment best fits into your program.

The Integrated Unit Portfolio

Many teachers have moved toward a more holistic approach to instruction that uses inter-disciplinary or integrated units of study. Assessment, therefore, should also become holistic. Portfolios lend themselves beautifully to this approach. Theme-related learning activities that span several subject areas are assessed and compiled into one portfolio. You might do a portfolio on a theme-based science unit on the ocean. You might also have students compile a portfolio for a theme-based literature unit using a book such as *The Very Hungry Caterpillar.* Dinosaurs or teddy bears are excellent choices for thematic units in early childhood.

The Multi-Disciplinary Portfolio

If you are not using thematic units, you can still combine related subject areas into one portfolio. This is an efficient way to use the portfolio process and it help students see connections and relationships between subject areas. You might do a portfolio combining science and social studies. Student work might demonstrate relationships between weather and geography or species adaptation and geography. You might do a portfolio that compiles a variety of experiments using both math and science. Reading, writing, and language arts are easily combined. Try combining writing with a different subject area, such as creative arts or math. Students can write compositions about works of art or music. They can also explain in writing their mathematical calculations and reasoning.

However you decide to integrate portfolios, be sure to keep things organized with the contents lists provided on pages 39-43. You can staple the contents list to the front of the portfolio, tuck it inside, or place it in an acetate cover. Encourage students to set learning goals for each unit of study by completing the goal-setting record on page 44. Be sure they follow-up on the date chosen for goal completion. A generic cover suitable for early childhood portfolios is provided on page 45 if you choose not to design one specifically for each thematic unit. The student journal form, "Best Work" form, and "Personal Favorite" form are suitable for all types of portfolios.

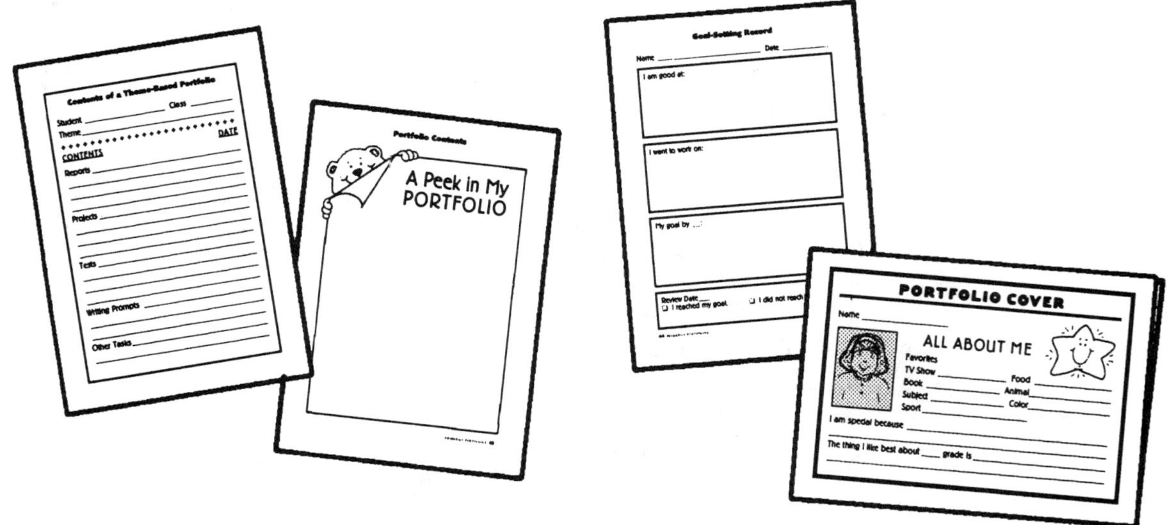

Contents of a Theme-Based Portfolio

Student ______________________ Class ____________

Theme ____

✦ ✦

CONTENTS DATE

Reports ____

____

____

____

Projects ____

____

____

____

Tests ____

____

____

____

Writing Prompts _________________________________

____

____

Other Tasks _____________________________________

____

Contents of an Early Childhood Unit Portfolio

Student_______________________________ Age________

Unit ________________ Teacher _____________________

✦ ✦

Language-Based Tasks Date

____

____

____

____

Fine and Gross Motor Tasks Date

____

____

____

____

____

Hands-On Math and Science Projects Date

____

____

____

____

Fine Arts and Creativity Date

____

____

____

____

Developmental Checklists Date

____

____

____

____

Social Skills Checklists or Activities Date

____

____

____

____

Other Tasks Date

____

____

Comments

____

____

Contents of a Multi-Disciplinary Portfolio

Student ______________________ Class ___________

Disciplines ______________________________________

✦ ✦

<u>CONTENTS</u> <u>DATE</u>

Projects

____

____

____

Tests and Checkpoints

____

____

____

Journals and Writing Tasks

____

____

____

Other Tasks

____

____

____

A Peek in My PORTFOLIO

Goal-Setting Record

Name ______________________________ Date ______________

I am good at:

I want to work on:

My goal by________________:

Review Date ________________

❑ I reached my goal. ❑ I did not reach my goal.

PORTFOLIO COVER

Name ____________________

(photo)

ALL ABOUT ME

Favorites

TV Show ________________ Food ________________

Book ________________ Animal ________________

Subject ________________ Color ________________

Sport ________________

I am special because ____

____

The thing I like best about _____ grade is ________________________________

____

Journal Form

My ______________________________ Journal

by _________________________

✦ ✦ ✦ ✦ ✦ ✦ ✦ ✦ ✦ ✦ ✦ ✦ ✦ ✦ ✦ ✦

I learned a lot about ________________________________

____

____

I really liked when we ______________________________

____

____

I want to find out more about _________________________

____

____

Draw a picture of what you learned.

This is my best work because...

____

____

____

____

Name ____________________

Date ____________________

This is my personal favorite because...

____

____

____

____

Name ____________________

Date ____________________

Student Contract

A contract can be helpful in keeping parents involved and making students feel important. Use this form at the beginning of the year to help students understand the seriousness of the effort you are expecting. Discuss how one shows respect for teachers, materials, and other students.

I, ____,

want to learn all that I can in school. I will work hard and listen to my teacher. I will take care of my portfolio and be sure to date all my work. I will show respect for other students and teachers and use materials with care.

Student ________________________________

Teacher ________________________________

Parent ________________________________

Date__________________________________

Language Arts and Reading

"Children need time for messing around with words."
JOHN HOLT

If portfolio assessment is a new endeavor and you seek to begin in one specific area, reading and language arts is a natural choice. Many of these projects require work over time, editing, or revision. Keeping it all in a portfolio will impress students with the magnitude of their work. Be sure they keep an up-to-date table of contents stapled to the front or tucked inside. Portfolios are a wonderful tool for helping students learn organizational skills—provided they are supplied with the tools to keep organized.

What goes in a language arts and reading portfolio?

- ✦ Reading and story logs
- ✦ Original stories and poems
- ✦ Writing prompts
- ✦ Book reports
- ✦ Character Chats
- ✦ "My Best Work"
- ✦ "My Personal Favorite"
- ✦ Samples of daily work
- ✦ Audio tape of child's reading
- ✦ Student journal
- ✦ Handwriting progress samples
- ✦ Rubrics
- ✦ Skills checklists

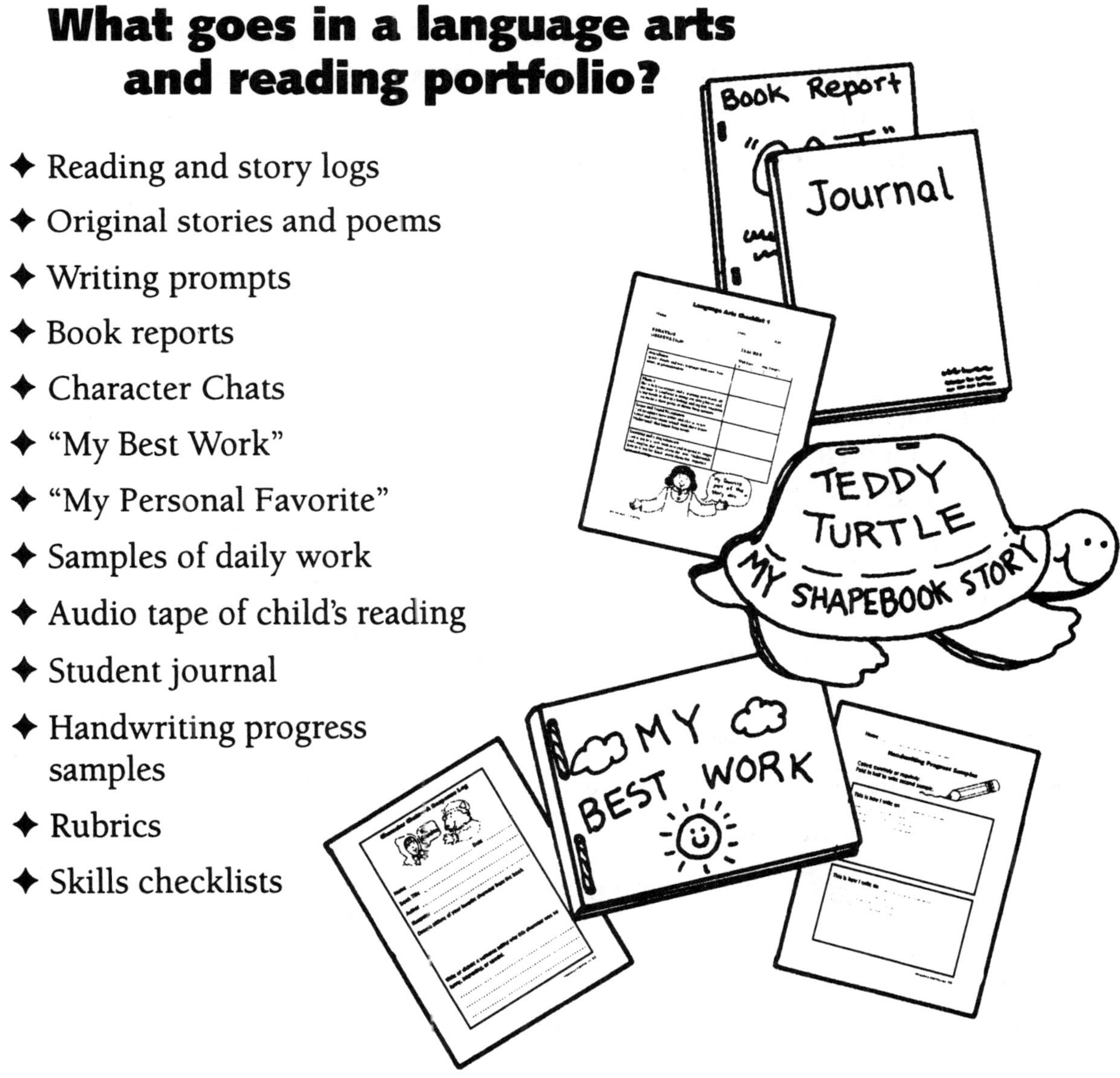

How can the primary teacher use these materials for effective language arts instruction?

In the primary grades, reading and language arts instruction receive a great deal of time and attention. This is entirely appropriate since language gives children the power to explore and question in many other areas of the curriculum. Research suggests that children who developed great talents or abilities later in life—whether they became musicians, scientists or writers—shared a love of books and reading. Words are powerful and children's literature provides an authentic context for those words. Consider the primary grade portfolio as a showcase for children's exploration of words. "Messing around with words" can mean dictating stories, being read to, listening to books on tape, reciting poems and rhymes, playing phonics games, forming word analogies, making class books, or practicing handwriting. Although portfolio assessment is normally linked with the whole language philosophy, it is possible to achieve a balance between phonics-based and literature-based instruction. Both give children important practice and experience in becoming readers and writers. Use portfolios to gather and showcase all sorts of reading and language tasks. Here are some guidelines for using portfolios to represent a valid picture of your instruction and your students' accomplishments.

- ✦ Students should be producing at least one piece of original writing each week. You might save one of these each month for the portfolio.
- ✦ Collect a "best product" handwriting sample each week.
- ✦ Save the vocabulary lists from each unit in the basal reader or the thematic unit and indicate which words the child can recognize.
- ✦ Save a weekly example of daily language drills on grammar and syntax.
- ✦ Keep a roster of children's pleasure reading selections.
- ✦ Save at least one example of oral language, such as an audio tape of the child reading aloud.

LANGUAGE ARTS
PORTFOLIO
Name

Reading and Story Log

Name______________________________ Grade____________

Title________________________________ Date____________

Parent or teacher______________________________________

My rating of this book (circle one) ★★★★ ★★★ ★★ ★

Title________________________________ Date____________

Parent or teacher______________________________________

My rating of this book (circle one) ★★★★ ★★★ ★★ ★

Title________________________________ Date____________

Parent or teacher______________________________________

My rating of this book (circle one) ★★★★ ★★★ ★★ ★

Character Chats—A Response Log

Name ______________________ Date ____________

Book Title ______________________________

Author ______________________________

Illustrator ______________________________

Draw a picture of your favorite character from the book.

Write or dictate a sentence telling why this character was so funny, interesting, or special.

____

____

____

More Character Chats

Name ______________________________ Date ____________

Directions: Use this as a follow-up to **Character Chats—A Response Log.**

List three adjectives that describe the way your favorite character looks.

_________________ _________________ _________________

List three adjectives that describe the way your favorite character behaves.

_________________ _________________ _________________

If you could ask the character one question, what would it be?

____

____

____

Tell why you would or would not want this character for a best friend.

____

____

____

Sample Writing Prompt

Name ______________________________ Date ____________

A POEM ABOUT ME

Follow these directions to write a special poem about you. You can read the directions or listen as your teacher reads them.

Line One: Write your first name.
Line Two: Write three words that describe how you are special.
Line Three: Write a sentence that names your favorite person.
Line Four: Write a sentence about something that you like to do for fun.
Line Five: Write a sentence about your favorite kind of book.
Line Six: Write a sentence about your favorite color.
Line Seven: Write your last name.

A POEM ABOUT ME

1. ______________________________

2. ______________________________

3. ______________________________

4. ______________________________

5. ______________________________

6. ______________________________

7. ______________________________

Sample Descriptive Writing Prompt

Name ______________________________ Date ____________

Tell about the best birthday you ever had. You might describe a party or just a special day with your mom, dad, or grandparents. What did you do? Why was this day so special? Give lots of details about your special birthday.

My ___________ birthday was the best one because

____

____

____

____

Draw a picture of the best birthday cake to go with your story.

Name ______________________________

Handwriting Progress Samples

Collect quarterly or regularly.
Fold in half to write second sample.

This is how I write on ____________________
(date)

____

____

____

____

This is how I write on ____________________
(date)

____

____

____

____

Language Arts and Reading Assessment

Once the projects or products have been gathered into a portfolio, the time has come for assessment. There are many ways to approach the task and all are valid—as long as you are organized and consistent. You may choose to evaluate the body of work as a whole. You may choose to evaluate each individual project in a "Best Products" portfolio. Or you and the student may choose items for assessment from a "Work in Progress" portfolio. Impress frequently upon your students that it is crucial that all work be date-stamped if growth over time is to be observed. You may choose to observe this growth weekly, bi-weekly, monthly, or some other way. You may set up a rolling schedule of assessment for your class or do the entire class at one or two sittings. Use rubrics and checklists similar to the examples that follow or design your own once you are familiar with their use. Letter grades have been indicated in parentheses if your school requires them.

Reading Rubric 1

4 *Outstanding Performance (Grade of A)*
Student recognizes letters and can associate sounds with letters (phonics). He or she has begun to recognize high-frequency "sight" words and to write these words in stories. In most situations, the student can read independently and enjoys reading both aloud and silently. Student uses words and language with great fluency and flexibility and demonstrates a high level of understanding of the plots and characters in literature.

3 *Competent Performance (Grade of B)*
Student recognizes letters and also associates the appropriate sound with the letter. He or she may recognize some high-frequency "sight" words and may also be able to write these words in stories. Student is ready to begin formal reading instruction and also enjoys both being read to and "reading" books independently. He or she can explain a basic story plot.

2 *Satisfactory Performance (Grade of C)*
Student is making progress in recognizing letters and in associating sounds with letters. He or she needs prompting to relate the details of a story. Child may enjoy books at times but probably prefers other kinds of learning-play. He or she is not ready for independent reading and requires more practice with basic skills and engagement in listening and speaking activities.

1 *Special Assistance Recommended (No grade)*
Student is not making adequate progress for his or her age and developmental level. A conference is recommended to discuss special assistance.

Reading Rubric 2

4 *Outstanding Performance (Grade of A)*
Student is reading independently and chooses books that challenge his or her ability. Comprehension skills, such as inferencing, word meaning, and sequencing, are handled with ease. Child brings eagerness and flexibility to the reading experience. He or she has mastered a large vocabulary and uses this in both reading and language activities.

3 *Competent Performance (Grade of B)*
Student is reading with ease, although he or she occasionally needs assistance from an adult. Comprehension skills, such as inferencing, word meaning, and sequencing, usually offer little trouble, although student typically relies on "looking back" to remember details. He or she has a good vocabulary but may not be highly creative or flexible in use of language.

2 *Satisfactory Performance (Grade of C)*
Student can read but still takes time to sound out many words. He or she requires assistance on a regular basis. This student needs prompting in order to respond to reading comprehension questions and may not be confident in completing these tasks. Student may not enjoy reading for pleasure and needs guidance choosing books that are appealing.

1 *Special Assistance Needed (No grade)*
Student is having a hard time learning to read. Problems with auditory or visual memory and/or inability to pay attention to details get in the way of his or her progress. Special testing may be in order to determine the extent and cause of the reading delay.

Language Arts Checklist 1

Name ______________________________ Date ___________ Age _______

BEHAVIOR	TEACHER OBSERVATION *With Ease.........Has Trouble* 4 3 2 1
Articulation Speaks clearly and uses language with ease. Few errors in pronunciation.	_____
Fluency Has a rich vocabulary and is learning new words all the time. Is comfortable trying out new phrases and using words to describe feelings and explain situations. Can recite a short poem or rhyme from memory.	_____
Letter and Sound Recognition Can recognize most letters and also associate vowel and consonant sounds with these letters. Understands that letters form words.	_____
Listening and Comprehension Can listen to a story with ease and respond to simple and complex questions about the story. Understands how to listen for details about characters, sequence, plot, and setting.	_____

Language Arts Checklist 2

Name ______________________________ Date ___________ Age _______

BEHAVIOR	TEACHER OBSERVATION *With Ease.........Has Trouble* 4 3 2 1
Mechanics Uses grammar and punctuation appropriately. Work is free of most spelling errors.	_____
Comprehension and Inferencing Demonstrates a high level of understanding of a story or text. Can report details and make inferences about character, plot, and setting.	_____
Vocabulary and Speech Uses a rich, diverse vocabulary and speaks clearly. Is learning new words and uses multiple-meaning words. Speech contains no frequent grammatical errors and shows no articulation problems.	_____
Reading Reads well for his or her age and grade. Is eager to read and chooses challenging books.	_____
Handwriting Is neat and well-formed.	_____

Language Arts Checklist 2

Name *Megan Anderson* Date *2-7-95* Age *7yr. 1 mo.*

BEHAVIOR	TEACHER OBSERVATION *With Ease.........Has Trouble* 4 3 2 1
Mechanics Uses grammar and punctuation appropriately. Work is free of most spelling errors.	2 Frequent spelling errors- letter reversals. Recommend vision check.
Comprehension and Inferencing Demonstrates a high level of understanding of a story or text. Can report details and make inferences about character, plot, and setting.	4 Very sharp! Comes up with interesting answers to story questions.
Vocabulary and Speech Uses a rich, diverse vocabulary and speaks clearly. Is learning new words and uses multiple-meaning words. Speech contains no frequent grammatical errors and shows no articulation problems.	4 Megan is extremely verbal - very lively and clear conversation.
Reading Reads well for his or her age and grade. Is eager to read and chooses challenging books.	3 Some problems here- may be related to letter reversals
Handwriting Is neat and well-formed.	4-3 Megan needs to slow down and work a bit more carefully here.

Mathematics

"It is not enough to have a good mind; the main thing is to use it well."

RENÉ DESCARTES

The use of a portfolio for mathematics invites the application of other skills—particularly writing—to the subject area. Rather than simply a collection of skill sheets, a mathematics portfolio may also include a collection of thoughts and observations by the student that relate to the world of numbers and calculations as well as a variety of other activities as suggested below.

What goes in a math portfolio?

- Quizzes
- Timed skills tests
- Math storyboard activities
- Pattern-making activities
- Original books about counting and sorting
- Math Chats
- "My Best Work"
- "My Personal Favorite"
- Student journal
- Estimating sheets
- Rubrics
- Skills checklists

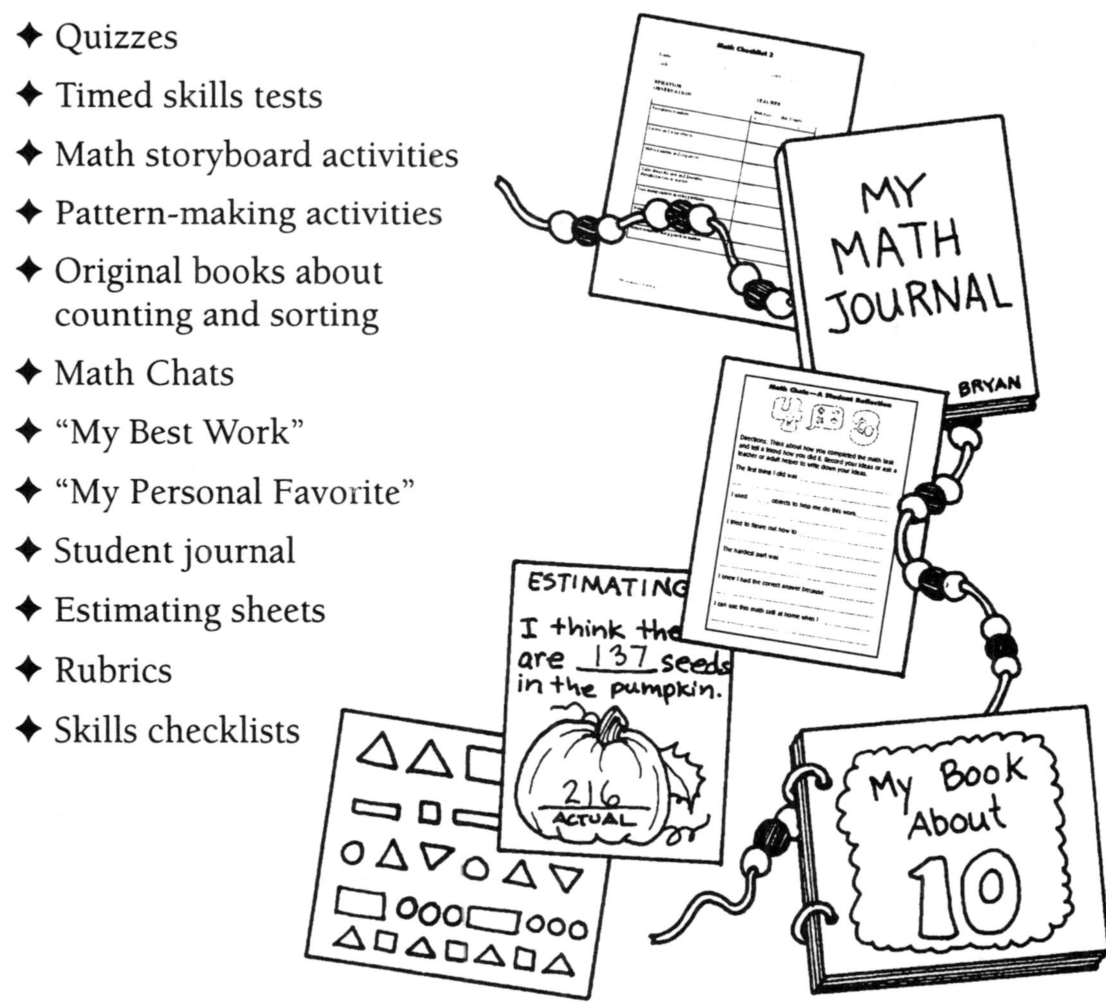

How can the primary teacher use these materials for effective math instruction?

✦ Don't isolate math from language instruction. Talk with young children about counting, sorting, estimating, and patterning. Think of numbers as a special kind of language for describing the world.

✦ Use manipulatives to build a foundation for more abstract tasks later. Match them to your thematic unit. Animal crackers, jelly beans, pumpkin seeds, colored beads, old keys, spools, cereal rings, and buttons make great manipulatives.

✦ Gather math activities for the portfolio that demonstrate both basic skills and higher-order thinking skills.

✦ Remember that drill and practice have an important role in instruction. Don't neglect them yet don't make them the centerpiece of your academic table.

✦ Relate math to real-life situations. Cooking, using maps, reading movie schedules, telling time, setting places at the table, estimating the number of seeds in a pumpkin—all make math practical and primary.

✦ Be sure to display math activities and papers frequently and with flair. See pages 19-30 for display ideas.

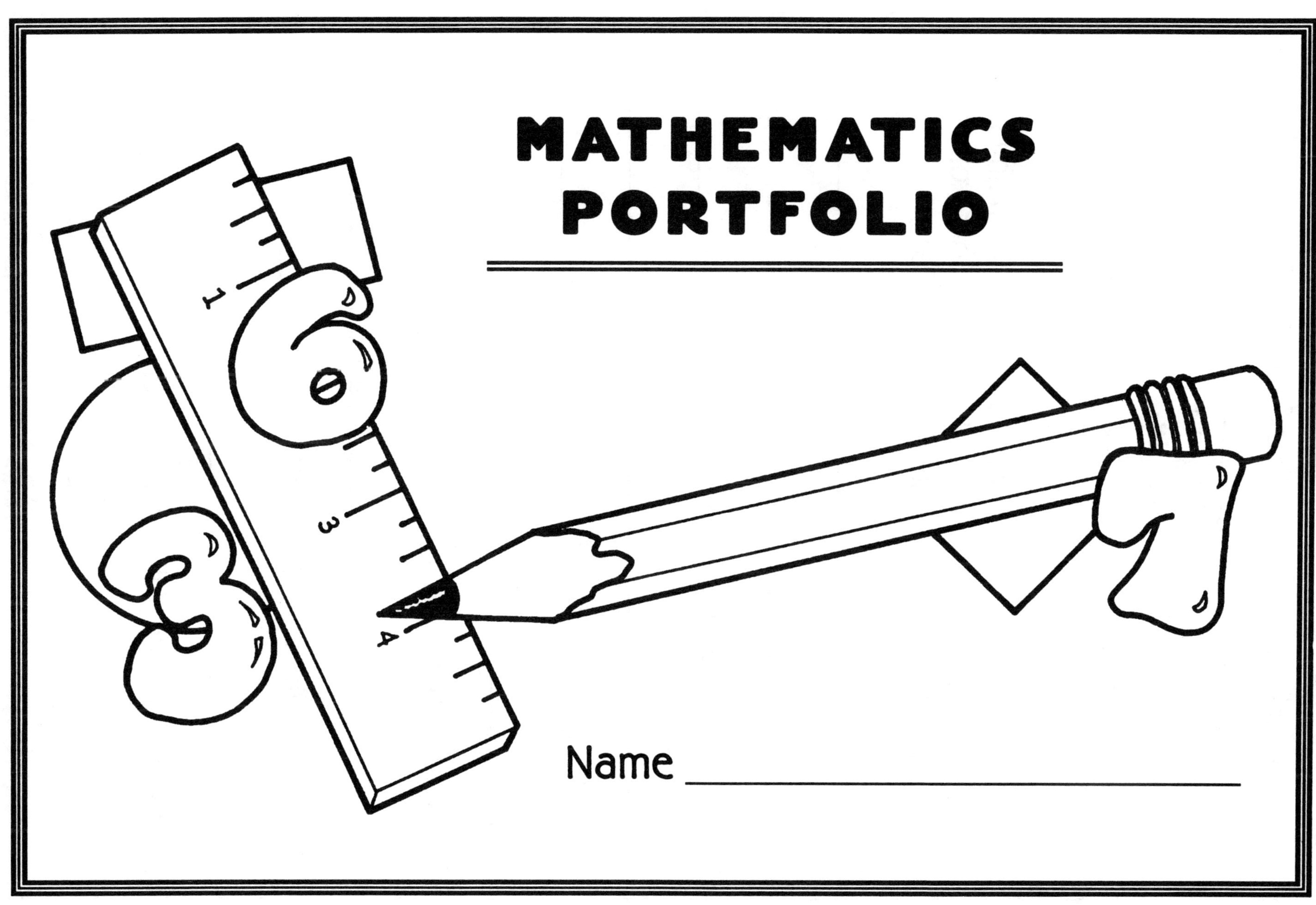
MATHEMATICS
PORTFOLIO
1
3
4
Name

Math Chats—A Student Reflection

Directions: Think about how you completed the math task and tell a friend how you did it. Record your ideas or ask a teacher or adult helper to write down your ideas.

The first thing I did was ______________________________

____

I used _______ objects to help me do this work.__________

____

I tried to figure out how to _________________________

____

The hardest part was ____________________________

____

I knew I had the correct answer because _____________

____

I can use this math skill at home when I _____________

____

Math Storyboards

Use the following open-ended storyboards to give a pictorial view of a math task. This can be done through illustration, magazine cut-outs, stamps, or stickers. Place this storyboard in the portfolio, along with a description of the task and a rubric of the performance. You may also use storyboards with manipulatives, such as small crackers, jelly beans, gummy bears, or plastic animals, for a practice session or skill refresher. Then let the children use colorful stickers, magazine cut-outs, or original artwork to show how a math task was solved. The storyboards can be duplicated on colored paper to match a theme or laminated to be used with washable markers at an activity center.

Math Storyboard

Beary Good Counting Board

Sample Storyboard Task

Objective

Students will demonstrate auditory memory skills, counting skills, and problem solving using manipulatives.

Materials

- ✦ Beary Good storyboard and small paper cup for each child containing ten small teddy bear crackers
- ✦ *Corduroy the Bear* by Don Freeman

Procedure

Read the story *Corduroy the Bear* aloud to the children. During center time or in small groups, do the storyboard lesson that follows. Have children use the teddy bear crackers to solve the problems. Use the checklist on page 77 for assessment. This activity can be adapted to any bear story you choose. It works best with small groups of 4 to 6 students at a round table or one-on-one.

Corduroy wandered into the toy department and met three more bears. Show me how many bears are in the toy department now.

(Students should place four bear crackers on storyboard)

Did you place four bears on the storyboard? Very good.

Now let's imagine that a little boy comes in to choose a teddy bear for his best friend. How many will be left on the shelf?

(Students remove one cracker, leaving three)

Did you leave three bears on the storyboard? Great!

The three bears decided to leave the store and ride the bus down to the zoo. At the bear habitat, they found two big bears and one small bear.

How many bears are at the zoo altogether?

(Students should have six bears on the storyboard)

Well, these six bears became good friends and decided to live together at the zoo. But there was one problem. The bear habitat was just big enough for five bears. How many will have to move out?

You're right! One bear will have to leave the zoo.

Now I want you to take the bear who moved out and place him back in the cup. Count the bears that are now in the cup. How many do you have?

(Students should have five bears in the cup)

Do you have more, fewer, or the same number of bears in the cup as you have left in the "zoo?"

Good! You have the same number in both places. Another word for the same number is "equal."

Now you can eat your bear crackers.

Use this generic estimating response form for all kinds of estimating activities in the primary classroom.

Name ______________________________ Date ____________

ESTIMATING SHEET

My best guess is ____

I made this guess because ______________________________

____

Here is a picture of what I was thinking about when I made my guess.

Teacher's Comments ______________________________________

____

____

Sample Math Task

Objective

The children will measure familiar objects to the nearest inch using a ruler. They will then determine how many of some of the items will fit within certain others.

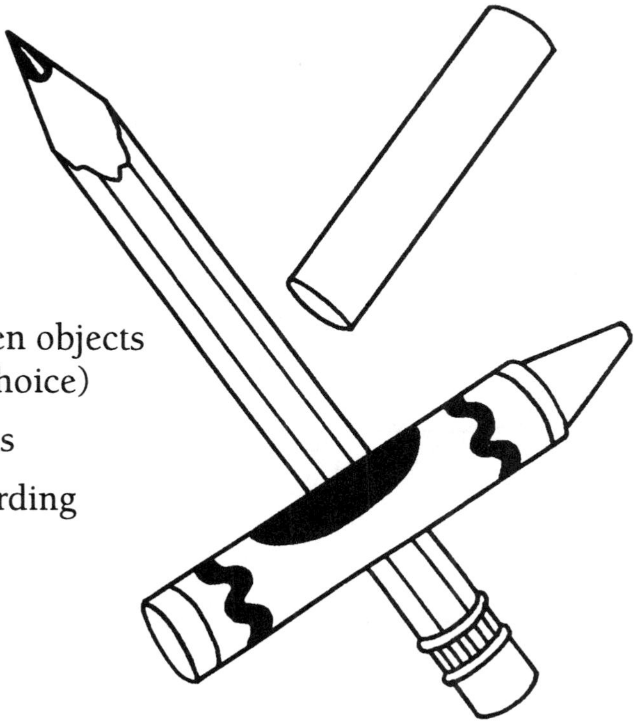

Materials

- book
- pencil
- lunch box
- shoe
- chalkboard
- notebook
- crayon
- glue bottle
- poster
- key
- (or any ten objects of your choice)
- clipboards
- data recording sheets
- rulers

Procedure

Children will work in pairs. Place the ten objects in various locations around the room. Students will take turns measuring objects and recording data on the recording sheet. They may not move any of the items to another location. Give a signal when it is time for partners to move to the next object—three minutes should be ample time. Once they have measured every item, partners can choose a quiet place in which to work on the second part of the task. You may choose to have them use calculators. Use the math checklist on page 76 to evaluate student work.

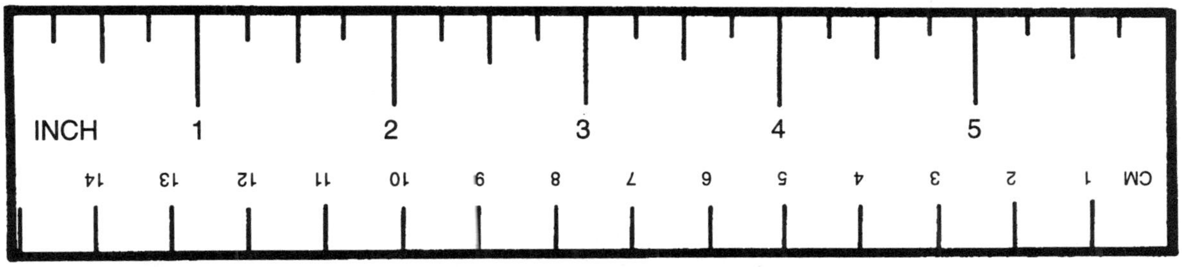

Names ______________________________ Date ______________

____

DATA RECORDING SHEET

	Object	Measurement
1.	______________________	______________________
2.	______________________	______________________
3.	______________________	______________________
4.	______________________	______________________
5.	______________________	______________________
6.	______________________	______________________
7.	______________________	______________________
8.	______________________	______________________
9.	______________________	______________________
10.	______________________	______________________

Now answer the following questions according to your measurements.

1. Will the book fit into the lunch box?______
2. Will six posters fit in one row across the chalkboard without overlapping?______
3. What is the size difference between the pencil and the glue bottle?______
4. How many keys long is the shoe?______
5. Would three crayons lined up end-to-end be longer than the notebook?______

Mathematics Assessment

You may choose to assess the contents of a mathematics portfolio in the same way you handle a language arts portfolio assessment (see page 58). Or you might decide to design a specific task for assessment, such as the measuring exercise on page 73, to be included in the portfolio with other work. Try for a "real-life" task that demonstrates math application outside the classroom walls.

Math Rubric

4 *Outstanding Performance*

- Completes task without assistance
- Demonstrates flexibility in thinking
- Solves problems with 90% or better accuracy
- Uses verbal or artistic skills creatively in solving problems

3 *Competent Performance*

- Completes task with minimal assistance
- Demonstrates understanding of math concepts
- Solves problems with 80% to 89% accuracy

2 *Passing Performance*

- Needs frequent help to complete the task
- Needs more time to develop understanding of concept
- Solves problems with less than 80% accuracy

1 *Unacceptable Performance/Needs Reteaching*

- Does not demonstrate adequate understanding of math concepts required in task

Math Checklist 1

Name______________________________ Date ______________

Task____

BEHAVIOR	TEACHER OBSERVATION *Outstanding.........Reteach* 4 3 2 1
Meets district objectives for math	______
Understands the concept and applies it to real-life situations	______
Can verbally explain how he or she solved problem or designed task	______
Works with diligence and confidence	______
Finds the correct answer	______
Recognizes the relationship of this concept to other math concepts	______

Math Checklist 2

Name_________________________________ Date ______________

Task ____

BEHAVIOR	TEACHER OBSERVATION *With Ease.........Has Trouble* 4 3 2 1
Recognizes numbers	_____
Counts and sorts objects	_____
Makes patterns and sequences	_____
Talks about the task and describes thought process to teacher	_____
Uses manipulatives to solve problems	_____
Estimates an answer or amount	_____
Writes numbers using pencil or marker	_____

Math Checklist 2

Name Cody Stanley Date 10-22-94

Task Bear Storyboard Problems (5 yr. 2 mo.)

BEHAVIOR	TEACHER OBSERVATION *With Ease.........Has Trouble* 4 3 2 1
Recognizes numbers	N/A
Counts and sorts objects	4 Counted aloud and used crackers - no errors
Makes patterns and sequences	2 Somewhat random in this regard - may need work on organizational skills
Talks about the task and describes thought process to teacher	4 Offered answers - seemed eager to move ahead.
Uses manipulatives to solve problems	4 Cody seemed confident in his ability to solve problems using crackers.
Estimates an answer or amount	3 Hesitant to offer estimates without use of manipulatives
Writes numbers using pencil or marker	N/A

Science and Social Studies

"But observation alone is not enough.
We have to understand the significance of what we see, hear, and touch."
JOHN DEWEY

Science and social studies can share a portfolio or you can separate them—whatever works best for your program. Use portfolios to collect work in which students apply concepts and knowledge they have gleaned through experimentation or interview, researched in the library, or produced for themselves through creative projects. Allow for lots of inquiry and exploration in both subject areas.

What goes in a science or social studies portfolio?

- ✦ Glossary of terms
- ✦ Student journals
- ✦ Drawings and observations
- ✦ Maps drawn by children
- ✦ Tests
- ✦ Science or Social Studies Chats
- ✦ "My Best Work"
- ✦ "My Personal Favorite"
- ✦ Book reports
- ✦ Tasks and group projects
- ✦ Rubrics
- ✦ Teacher checklists

How can the primary teacher use these materials for effective science and social studies instruction?

For observation to become understanding, students must manipulate facts in situations with real-life applications. Since all of science and social studies is about real life, this should not be difficult to achieve. However, all too often, students' learning remains at the knowledge level of Bloom's taxonomy—no application or synthesis ever takes place. Enrich science and social studies experiences for your students with some of the following ideas.

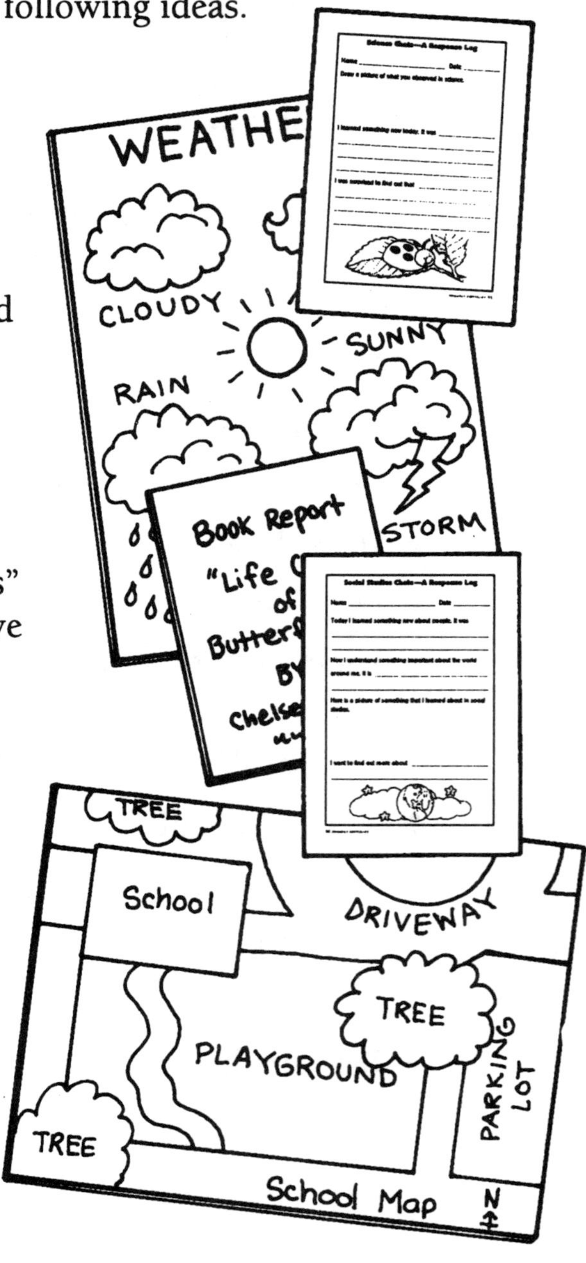

- ✦ Supply a basic glossary of terms for each new unit but encourage students to add their own newly-discovered terminology. Be sure they have an opportunity to demonstrate understanding of the words through a writing assignment or a dictated story.
- ✦ Use a generic journal form or develop a format especially for science or social studies. Be sure to include a space for illustration of a concept or phenomenon. "Science Chats" and "Social Studies Chats" invite students to reflect on what they have observed.
- ✦ Primary children love maps. Capitalize on their fascination by having a supply of all kinds of maps in your classroom. Be sure there are maps of both familiar and unfamiliar places. Invite students to reflect on what a world without maps would be like. Have them draw maps of real and imagined territories.
- ✦ Combine reading with science or social studies through non-fiction book reports in these areas. Your librarian or media specialist will have plenty of suggestions.

SCIENCE PORTFOLIO
COVER
Name

SOCIAL STUDIES
PORTFOLIO COVER
Name

Science Chats—A Response Log

Name ______________________________ Date ____________

Draw a picture of what you observed in science.

I learned something new today. It was ____________________

____

____

____

I was surprised to find out that _________________________

____

____

____

Social Studies Chats—A Response Log

Name ______________________________ Date ____________

Today I learned something new about people. It was

____

____

Now I understand something important about the world

around me. It is ______________________________________

____

Here is a picture of something that I learned about in social studies.

I want to find out more about __________________________

____

Sample Science Task

Objective

Students will analyze objects to determine which are living and which are non-living.

Materials

- ✦ quart-size plastic zipper bags
- ✦ chart paper
- ✦ brown and green markers
- ✦ smooth work surface
- ✦ two plastic dishpans or boxes
- ✦ magnifying glasses
- ✦ *My Big Book of the Outdoors* by Jane Werner Watson or any children's story that describes a variety of natural objects, both living and non-living.

Procedure

1. Begin the lesson with an open-ended question, such as, "How do we know if things in nature are living or non-living?"
2. Introduce the story, read it aloud, and repeat the original question for discussion.
3. Include in the discussion such concepts in nature as color, function, movement, eating, and breathing as they relate to living and non-living objects.
4. Take a walk with the students around the school grounds if appropriate, or around a local park. Students will work in pairs to pick up at least five objects found in nature. Objects can be placed in plastic bags for easy transit back to the classroom.
5. After returning to the classroom, invite students to examine the objects using a magnifying glass when appropriate. Students can classify objects as either living or non-living by placing them in the designated box or dishpan.
6. With the entire class, discuss whether objects are living or non-living. Record responses on chart paper using a green marker for living items and a brown marker for non-living items.
7. Invite students to complete Science Chats—A Response Log on page 83 for inclusion in their portfolios. Use the science rubric on page 88 and the checklist on page 89 for assessment.

Sample Social Studies Task

WHAT'S GOING ON?

Directions:

Cut and paste a current events article from a magazine or newspaper in the space below. Use markers to indicate important information.

- ✦ Use a red marker to circle the name of the most important person in the event.
- ✦ Use a green marker to draw a box around the place where the event happened.
- ✦ Use a blue marker to underline the date of the event.
- ✦ Now write at least two sentences on the back of your paper telling why this event is important for people to know about.

Science and Social Studies Assessment

The information on language arts and reading assessment on page 58 applies to science and social studies as well. However, you are more likely to be using a "Best Products" or unit format for these subject areas since development in science and social studies is not necessarily linear. Or you may choose to design an assessment task that asks students to apply what they have learned. Decide what skills are important to assess before you design the task and try to give students more than one opportunity to display the skill.

Science Rubric

4 *Outstanding Performance*
Demonstrates keen skills in observation and data gathering. Can see and discuss similarities and differences in science. Key vocabulary is used with confidence. Is eager to experiment and discuss findings of experiments. Readily connects science concepts to real-life experiences and other areas of the curriculum. Looks for new and creative ways to use materials in science.

3 *Competent Performance*
Demonstrates ability to observe and gather data with some prompting. Is able to compare and contrast science experiences. Key vocabulary used approximately. Follows directions with experiments and answers questions about observations. Relates science to real-life situations with assistance.

2 *Satisfactory Performance*
Is learning to observe and gather data. Can define terms and respond to questions using those terms. Can participate in experiments with assistance and is beginning to connect science to the real world.

1 *Assistance Needed*
Has not demonstrated an adequate understanding of the scientific process. Has not mastered key vocabulary. Has not developed skills in observation or data collection.

Science Checklist

Name____________________________ Date ____________

Unit ______________ Teacher ________________________

BEHAVIOR	TEACHER OBSERVATION *With Ease.........Has Trouble* 4 3 2 1
Observation Uses all the senses to explore life, earth, and physical science.	______
Inquiry Demonstrates curiosity and delight in science. Wants to know "why" and thinks of lots of ways to find out.	______
Collects Data Makes lists. Charts growth. Draws and sketches. Fills in graphs and charts.	______
Research Skills Uses a glossary and other written materials to gather information. Can do simple reports and searches.	______
Experiments Manipulates materials with care. Follows directions. Looks for patterns and changes.	______

Science Checklist

Name Lauren Warrington Date 3-7-95

Task Thematic Unit – "The Ocean"

BEHAVIOR	TEACHER OBSERVATION *With Ease.........Has Trouble* 4 3 2 1
Observation Uses all the senses to explore life, earth, and physical science.	4 Did a beautiful job on her first print
Inquiry Demonstrates curiosity and delight in science. Wants to know "why" and thinks of lots of ways to find out.	4 Asked excellent questions on aquarium trip - says she wants to be a scientist!
Collects Data Makes lists. Charts growth. Draws and sketches. Fills in graphs and charts.	4+ Lauren's sea shell graph showed skill and neatness - very advanced.
Research Skills Uses a glossary and other written materials to gather information. Can do simple reports and searches.	4 Chose high level books during free reading time
Experiments Manipulates materials with care. Follows directions. Looks for patterns and changes.	3 "Ocean in a Jar" made correctly but somewhat hastily - Lauren is sometimes over-confident!

Social Studies Rubric

4 *Outstanding Performance*
Uses key vocabulary with confidence and can explain observations in spoken or written form. Relates geography, history, political science, and civics to real-life situations. Demonstrates age-appropriate skill in using maps and globe. Uses social studies concepts to understand the world around him or her. Moves beyond understanding to explore creative solutions for problems in the community and world at large.

3 *Competent Performance*
Can define key vocabulary. Can answer questions involving geography, history, political science, or civics with prompting. Is becoming confident in map and globe skills. Is using social studies to understand the world around him or her.

2 *Satisfactory Performance*
Gaining confidence in using key vocabulary. Making progress in understanding key concepts in geography, history, political science, and civics. Is becoming familiar with use of maps and globe.

1 *Assistance Needed*
Has not demonstrated an acceptable level of understanding of vocabulary and concepts under study.

Social Studies Checklist

Name__________________________________ Date _______________

Unit _________________ Teacher ______________________________

BEHAVIOR	TEACHER OBSERVATION *With Ease.........Has Trouble* 4 3 2 1
Geography Recognizes and names key land masses and bodies of water. Names major cities and states in proximity to own town. Understands concepts of place and climate.	_____
History Names famous Americans and associates them with events and places.	_____
Civics Can recite Pledge of Allegiance and discuss basic concepts of democracy. Understands the concept of voting and political leadership. Can name current U.S. president and mayor of own town.	_____
Cultural Geography Describes food, clothing, holidays, and traditions from several cultures. Recognizes the value of different cultures.	_____

Social Studies Checklist

Name Mark Sun Ling* Date 12-10-94

Unit The Community Teacher K. Smith

BEHAVIOR *Thai is student's primary language	TEACHER OBSERVATION *With Ease.........Has Trouble* 4 3 2 1
Geography Recognizes and names key land masses and bodies of water. Names major cities and states in proximity to own town. Understands concepts of place and climate.	3 Uses state and local maps to become more familiar– making good progress.
History Names famous Americans and associates them with events and places.	2 Language barrier makes this a bit of a challenge– using peer partner for review
Civics Can recite Pledge of Allegiance and discuss basic concepts of democracy. Understands the concept of voting and political leadership. Can name current U.S. president and mayor of own town.	3 Participates eagerly in morning exercises
Cultural Geography Describes food, clothing, holidays, and traditions from several cultures. Recognizes the value of different cultures.	4 Shares Thai culture with pride. Enjoys pointing out areas of similarity and difference.

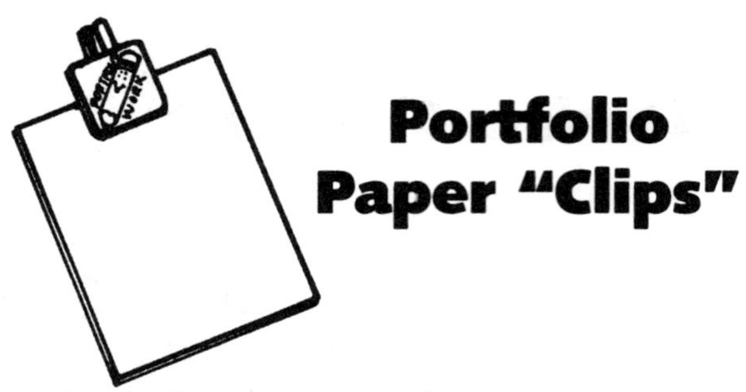

Portfolio Paper "Clips"

Reproduce these designs on oaktag or construction paper for children to color and cut out. Laminate if possible for greater durability. Print each child's name on four spring-type clothespins and glue to the back of their colored designs. Use to hold or display portfolio work.

Portfolio Fold-overs

Reproduce the fold-overs below and cut apart. Staple to packets of student work you send home that is to be returned for inclusion in the portfolio.

WORK
PORTFOLIO

Please look these papers over and sign below.

Return by ____________

____

WORK
PORTFOLIO

Please return to school by

____

This is for my portfolio.

WORK
PORTFOLIO

Please look these papers over and sign below.

Return by ____________

____

WORK
PORTFOLIO

Please return to school by

____

This is for my portfolio.

Portfolio Party

Celebrate the success of your students and thank the volunteers who helped you by throwing a gala portfolio party at the end of the year. Display as much student work as possible—particularly on the "Sweet Success" bulletin board (see page 29). Invite other classes and members of the administration to view student work and hear students' presentations. Encourage students to design portfolio placemats on open manila file folders. Serve "portfolio sandwiches" using pita pockets trimmed into rectangles with a hinge on one side. Provide a variety of fillings and condiments so students can make their own portfolio sandwiches. Duplicate the badge pattern and personalize it for each student. Encourage student suggestions for other ways to celebrate their successes.